KUNG POW CHICKEN★

HEROES ON THE SIDE

Cyndi Marko

BRANCHES
SCHOLASTIC INC.

For Lucian
Guess what? Chicken butt

No part of this publication may be reproduced, stored in a retrieval system, or transmitted in any form or by any means, electronic, mechanical, photocopying, recording, or otherwise, without written permission of the publisher. For information regarding permission, write to Scholastic Inc., Attention: Permissions Department, 557 Broadway, New York, NY 10012.

Library of Congress Cataloging-in-Publication Data
Marko, Cyndi, author, illustrator.
Heroes on the side / by Cyndi Marko.
pages cm. — (Kung Pow Chicken ; 4)
Summary: When the Blue family travels to New Yolk City, Egg Drop wants to go to the first-ever Sidekick Super-Con—a big party for sidekicks—but Ticklebeak and his Bad Eggs soon chicknap the sidekicks and it is up to Kung Pow Chicken to save them.
ISBN 0-545-61074-5 (pbk.) — ISBN 0-545-61077-X (hardcover) — ISBN 0-545-61395-7 (ebook) [1. Superheroes—Fiction. 2. Chickens—Fiction. 3. Kidnapping—Fiction. 4. Humorous stories.] I. Title.
PZ7.M33968Her 2014
[Fic]—dc23
2014017066

ISBN 978-0-545-61077-3 (hardcover) / ISBN 978-0-545-61074-2 (paperback)

10 9 8 7 6 5 4 3 2 1   14 15 16 17 18 19/0

Printed in China
First Scholastic printing, December 2014

TABLE OF CONTENTS

pirate ship

first mate

city of Fowladelphia

pirate sword

comb

wattle

pirate sash

tail feathers

buried treasure (lunch box)

Gordon Blue seemed like an ordinary chicken.

Gordon had an ordinary family. (Most of the time.)

And he liked ordinary things.

My favorite comic.

I ♥ my bike.

I caught a fish!

But Gordon had a <u>super</u> secret.

Uncle Quack was the <u>only</u> chicken who knew Gordon's <u>super</u> secret. And everyone knew that Uncle Quack helped Kung Pow Chicken catch bad guys.

Gordon liked having superpowers. But it was <u>super</u> hard being a superhero.

Gordon's mom called when he was battling bad guys.

You're late!

Some people thought anyone could be a superhero.

And he had to put up with a cheeky sidekick.

I ♥ BEAKGIRL

Gordon loved chasing bad guys in his city. But today, the Blue family was getting ready to go on a trip to New Yolk City.

Gordon and Benny went to the lab to help their uncle pack.

Benny took the flyer from Uncle Quack.

SIDEKICK SUPER★CON!

Dear Egg Drop,

You are invited to a party! Radar, sidekick to NYC's Rubber Rooster, is proud to host the FIRST-EVER SIDEKICK SUPER-CON! Eat yummy lunch and dessert! Dance and play games with other sidekicks! And see who will win the SIDEKICK OF THE YEAR award!

★ **WHEN:** Saturday at 1 PM
★ ★ **WHERE:** Birdy Ballroom

Gordon and Benny went home to do their own packing.

The boys were too excited to sleep.

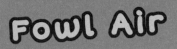

On Friday morning, the Blue family boarded a plane to New Yolk City!

Who says chickens can't fly?

FWOOSH!

FOWL AIR

They took a cab from the airport.

Hey, New Yolkers! It's a bit nippy in the Big Egg. If you've got a hat, wear it! In other news, bad-guy prankster Ticklebeak and a bunch of his Bad Eggs escaped from jail. Watch out for tricky chickens in striped pajamas. . . .

Nippy weather <u>and</u> bad guys?! Mom will <u>never</u> let us leave the hotel!

They all dropped off their luggage at the
Roostervelt Hotel.
    Then Mrs. Blue dashed off to the fancy shops.
And Uncle Quack took his nephews ice-skating.

They were all having fun on the ice.

Suddenly, Gordon's tail feathers started to tingle. He knew what that meant: A bad guy was up to no good!

The brothers found a good place to hide. Gordon flung open his lunch box and grabbed his super suit. Benny put on his mask.

Just then, <u>another</u> superhero team burst onto the ice.

Gordon squeezed into his leotard. But he was too late. Rubber Rooster and Radar had chased the bad guys away.

Rubber Rooster was swarmed by star-struck chickens. Kung Pow Chicken wanted to meet him. But he couldn't get through the crowd.

No one's ever asked you to sign anything.

New Yolk is Rubber Rooster's city. Let him catch the bad guys.

Gordon and Benny stayed in the hotel room for the rest of the day. Gordon moped. Benny daydreamed.

I'd like to thank Professor Quack. And my good friend Beak Girl.

Early Saturday morning, Gordon and his family
went sight-seeing all over New Yolk City.

Then it was almost time for Sidekick Super-Con! Uncle Quack had a plan to keep Mrs. Blue busy. He was taking her to the spa for an afternoon of pampering.

Benny was ready to go in a jiffy. But Gordon wanted to look <u>extra</u> super in case he ran into other superheroes.

By the time Gordon was ready, Benny was in a tizzy.

They rushed
out of the room
and down the
hall.

Gordon
hummed along
with the elevator
music.

Then they
scrambled
through the
lobby.

And the
doorman
hailed them
a cab.

BOK!

HOTEL

The cab headed to Sidekick Super-Con. Gordon was excited to visit the Statue of Libirdy after he dropped off Benny.

The cab zoomed in and out of traffic. Gordon and Benny bokked about the trapped sidekicks.

The cab skidded to a stop near the Birdy Ballroom. Gordon paid the taxi driver.

They put on their super suits.

Kung Pow Chicken jumped out, ready to battle! Egg Drop was already off and running.

4

Two Bad Eggs stood guard. The heroes tiptoed around the building to look for another way in.

Kung Pow Chicken slipped around the corner.
He crashed into another hero.

But Rubber Rooster and Kung Pow Chicken did not seem to notice Egg Drop. They had important <u>super</u> stuff to talk about.

Soon more superheroes showed up. They all had sidekicks trapped in the Birdy Ballroom.

While the superheroes were busy bokking, Ticklebeak and some Bad Eggs tried to sneak away. One of the Bad Eggs giggled.

The good guys got in a super-mega battle with the bad guys!

The battle raged on and on.

But the bad guys got away.

The other superheroes went off after the bad guys. But Kung Pow Chicken and Egg Drop were hungry.

The heroes ate pie and tried to figure out what to do next.

This pie is really good.

You've got berries on your beak.

RIIIING!!

Kung Pow Chicken answered his Beak-Phone.

It was Uncle Quack.

I have news! Ticklebeak's Bad Eggs are playing pranks all over the city! The other superheroes haven't been able to catch them! And the heroes' sidekicks are still trapped!

There's no way into that building! We'll need a gadget, Uncle Quack! Can you make something to help us get inside to rescue the sidekicks?

I'll get to work. Your mom is soaking in a mud bath. Oh! And the radio said no one has seen Ticklebeak.

We'll go where the Bad Eggs have already pranked. A clue could lead us to Ticklebeak! Can you find out more about him?

I'm on it! Good luck!

Kung Pow Chicken put away his phone.

39

The heroes rushed to the subway.

The Bad Eggs had been busy. They had hit all the hot spots in the city: the Statue of Libirdy, the New Yolk Public Library, and even Rockefeather Center.

First, Kung Pow Chicken and Egg Drop went to the Statue of Libirdy.

The Statue of Libirdy doesn't wear bloomers!

It's pretty funny though.

tee hee hee

The Bad Eggs had made a mess of the statue. But they hadn't left any clues to where Ticklebeak could be.

41

Next, the heroes went to the public library.

Then Kung Pow Chicken and Egg Drop went back to Rockefeather Center. Now the ice rink was filled with gooey white stuff.

The superheroes searched high and low. Finally, they spotted a clue.

As soon as the heroes reached the museum, Kung Pow Chicken's tail feathers started to tingle. Then Kung Pow Chicken and Egg Drop heard goofy giggling. They hid.

Ticklebeak and some Bad Eggs! What were they doing in the museum?

EGGENHEIM MUSEUM

giggle

giggle

Look! Ticklebeak has the Fancy-pants Gold Egg!

TINGLE!

45

Super-Silly String

Kung Pow Chicken and Egg Drop followed
Ticklebeak and the Bad Eggs all the way to
Times Oval.

Times Oval was full of Bad Eggs. They were making a mess.

Just then, the other superheroes showed up.
Kung Pow Chicken waved them over.

Egg Drop watched the superheroes fight with all their might.

Then he watched them all get caught! Without their sidekicks, the heroes were easily trapped.

A Bad Egg sprayed Kung Pow Chicken's beak shut with Super-Silly String.

Egg Drop had to free the superheroes. But he needed help. He needed sidekicks.

Egg Drop slipped away. He rushed back to the
hotel. Uncle Quack would know what to do.

Ticklebeak and his Bad Eggs
have chick-napped Gordon—and
the other superheroes, too! I'm
the <u>only</u> one who can save them!

And, um, I don't
think those cucumbers
are for eating.

HOTEL SPA
"FOR PUFFY
EYES"

Uncle Quack had been busy working on a new gadget.

This gadget should help you rescue the sidekicks. It's a super disguise called the Pi-ZZZ-a Guy™. I baked a yummy cheesy pizza. And I warmed a jug of milk. Together those should make those Bad Eggs super sleepy!

I'll keep your mom busy at the spa. Good luck.

Thanks!

Egg Drop pedaled the bicycle taxi to the Birdy Ballroom. Then he took a big breath and climbed up the front steps.

The Bad Eggs shrugged. They gobbled up the pizza. They gulped down the warm milk. Then their tummies were full and they fell asleep.

Egg Drop grabbed the key and unlocked the door.

The sidekicks were very happy to see Egg Drop.

Egg Drop had a plan. He told it to the sidekicks.

Then they took the subway to Times Oval.

The sidekicks burst up out of the subway.

They jumped right into battle with Ticklebeak's Bad Eggs.

Egg Drop and Radar slipped away from the fight. They ran over to free the superheroes. Egg Drop scraped the Super-Silly String from Kung Pow Chicken's beak.

Kung Pow, use your Power Peck!

PECK! PECK!

The superheroes were free of Ticklebeak's messy trap in no time.

Good work, Radar!

You, too, Egg Drop. But what took you so long? Now, let's get cracking!

The big battle continued. Then Ticklebeak stepped forward. He bokked loudly. Everyone stopped fighting so they could hear better.

But jail was no fun. Ticklebeak would not go back without a fight! Kung Pow Chicken flashed his Drumsticks of Doom.

The Bad Eggs rushed at the superheroes. The heroes were outnumbered.

But the sidekicks were ready! They tossed rolls of Ultra-Mega Toilet Paper to their superheroes. And they sprayed cans of Super-Silly String.

OF MICE AND CHICKENS

ZZZZZIP!

SPISH!

SPISH!

The sidekicks and superheroes put Ticklebeak and all of his Bad Eggs in one basket.

The good guys said their good-byes. Radar gave Egg Drop a high five.

Kung Pow Chicken and Egg Drop took off their super suits and ran back to the hotel.

Mrs. Blue gave her boys a big hug.

The next morning, the Blue family flew home to Fowladelphia. Gordon and Benny went with Uncle Quack to the lab. A surprise was waiting for Egg Drop.

WANTED

FOR BEING SILLY!

funny disguise

Cyndi Marko lives in Canada with her family.

When Cyndi was younger, she thought she was <u>so</u> funny. She loved to tell jokes to make her friends laugh. She would sneak up on her dad to scare him, giggling the whole time. And when guests came over, she would tell them her mom had made slime soup for dinner. (It was split green-pea soup! Pretty slimy, right? Ew!) Now that Cyndi is older, she—well, she still thinks she's pretty funny.

Kung Pow Chicken is Cyndi's first children's book series.

green slime soup

split peas

BIG BOOK OF JOKES

KUNG POW CHICKEN

Prove your superhero know-how!

Why does Gordon think it is super hard being a superhero?

Why does Ticklebeak make the Bad Eggs do pranks all over the city?

Draw pictures and write speech bubbles to retell the important events of <u>Heroes on the Side</u>.

How does Uncle Quack's gadget help Egg Drop rescue the sidekicks?

Egg Drop has just won the award for Sidekick of the Year. Write an acceptance speech for him!